THE ICE CREAM CONE

A Follett Beginning-To-Read Book
Level Three

THE ICE CREAM CONE

Mildred Wilds Willard

Illustrated by Jözef Sumichrast

FOLLETT PUBLISHING COMPANY
CHICAGO

Text copyright © 1973 by Mildred Wilds Willard. Illustrations copyright © 1973 by Follett Publishing Company, a division of Follett Corporation. All rights reserved. No part of this book may be reproduced in any form without written permission from the publisher. Manufactured in the United States of America.

ISBN 0-695-80418-9 Trade binding
ISBN 0-695-40418-0 Titan binding

Library of Congress Catalog Card Number: 73-81992

Fourth Printing

One long-ago summertime, a World's Fair was held in the city of St. Louis in Missouri.

People came from every state and from sixty countries. They came to see the new things. They came to show off their wares.

It happened that a boy named Jemal came to work at the fair. He was the helper of the baker, Mr. Hamwi. They had come from a country called Syria.

Jemal worked hard for Mr. Hamwi. They baked their sugar cakes on an open fire so that everyone could watch.

Mr. Hamwi's bake shop was next to an ice cream stand. Very soon, the ice cream man, named Frank, and the two cake bakers had become good friends.

When the busy day was done, they sat together and ate up their leftovers. Mr. Hamwi always had lots of leftover cake. Frank had to look in the very bottom of the can to find any leftover ice cream.

Most people passed right by the bake shop.
Instead, they stood in long lines to wait for ice cream.

One day Mr. Hamwi asked Jemal, "How can we
make these people buy our cakes?"

"I will call out," said Jemal. He called, "Taste
the treat baked special for the king's table!"

No one at the fair cared what a king ate.

Mr. Hamwi could smile no longer. He could not earn enough money to pay his rent. He was running out of flour and sugar.

So Mr. Hamwi told Jemal, "Go ask Frank for a job in his ice cream stand. He has work enough for two."

Jemal was sad for Mr. Hamwi, but he was glad to help his good friend, Frank.

That day the line was getting longer in front of the ice cream stand. A girl called out, "Hurry, please! Wait on me next or I'll miss the one hundred automobiles."

One hundred auto drivers had started their trip at New York City. They had crossed many states to get all the way to Missouri. Their long trip would end with a parade at the fair.

An automobile was a new invention. The fair
would be crowded with people who came to see the
one hundred automobiles. That's why Frank had
ordered six more cans of ice cream. That's why he
had ordered ten more boxes of paper dishes and
spoons from the paper factory.

Jemal and Frank worked faster and faster to wait on all the people. Everyone was in a hurry.

Jemal and Frank worked so fast that they bumped elbows. They reached again and again for paper dishes.

14

The pile of paper dishes grew smaller. Frank finally used the last dish. "We must make the people wait," he said. "I will get more paper dishes from the box in the back."

Frank looked through all the boxes in the back of his stand. Every box was empty. The new order had not come from the paper dish factory. Frank had been too busy to notice.

The factory was far away from the fair. Maybe the paper dishes had been lost on the way.

Out front Jemal waited for Frank to bring more paper dishes. The long line of people waited for ice cream. Some walked away frowning.

If Frank could not sell his ice cream, the sun would turn it into soup. The cans of ice cream were packed in ice. When the ice was melted, the ice cream would melt, too. But Frank could not sell one more scoop. He had to put a sign on the front of his stand that said CLOSED.

"Do you have any glass dishes?" Jemal asked.

"No," said Frank. "I could never wash glass dishes fast enough for all these people."

"Then I will find you some paper dishes," said Jemal. "This is a big fair. Surely someone will have some extra dishes."

"But not enough," said Frank sadly. "No one will have enough for all this ice cream."

First Jemal stopped at the cotton candy stand.

"I don't use paper dishes," said the cotton candy maker. "I put my candy on rolled-up pieces of paper."

21

The next place where Jemal stopped was full of bright lights.

"Come inside," said a man. "In here you will learn how the electric light was invented."

"I am looking for paper dishes now," said Jemal.

Suddenly, on the street right in front of Jemal, was a banging, popping thing. It was an automobile.

This driver was the first one to get to the fair from New York City. His long coat was dusty. He was wearing glasses and a cap.

"Come on!" said the driver. "I will give you a ride. Maybe you can help me find an ice cream stand."

"No, thank you," said Jemal. "I am looking for paper dishes. When I find some, you will be able to buy your ice cream at my friend's stand."

Jemal watched the auto go away. By now his feet hurt, and his head hurt, too. All the bright lights of the fair were whirling around and around. He closed his eyes and tried to wish for what he wanted.

Jemal opened his eyes. He saw no paper dishes, but he had something else to take back to Frank and Mr. Hamwi. He had a very good idea.

Jemal found Mr. Hamwi still in his shop, but he had stopped baking. The fire was almost out. The baking irons were cold. A sign that said CLOSED looked just like the sign on the ice cream stand.

Jemal smiled and picked up one of the cone-shaped cakes. Mr. Hamwi always filled these cones with honey and fruit to make a very special treat. Today he had not bothered to fill them with anything.

"Mr. Hamwi," said Jemal. "We are going to take this whole basket of cake cones to Frank. Today he will fill them with ice cream! Each cone will hold one scoop. If someone wants two scoops, the second scoop can be piled on top."

"It works! It works!" cried Frank when Jemal and Mr. Hamwi showed him how to sell his ice cream without paper dishes.

Then he said, "Stir up the fire and mix up more batter. I'll need as many sugar cakes as you can bake."

All that day Jemal ran back and forth between the bake shop and the ice cream stand. His elbows bumped Frank at the stand. His elbows bumped Mr. Hamwi in the bake shop. No one cared. They were all too happy.

"Tomorrow," said Mr. Hamwi, "let's put these two places together into one big business."

The next day and every day after that, long lines of people waited to buy the new ice cream treat. Everyone loved it.

Whenever there were any leftovers, Jemal liked a scoop of chocolate in his cone. Frank liked a scoop of strawberry. But Mr. Hamwi liked to pile up four scoops to make one of his extra-special ice cream cones.

The Ice Cream Cone

Reading Level: Level Three. *The Ice Cream Cone* has a total vocabulary of 312 words. It has been tested in third grade classes, where it was read with ease.

Uses of This Book: Reading for fun. Even though this story is made-up, it is based on an event that really happened—the ice cream cone was invented in 1904 at the World's Fair in St. Louis when a baker handed a cone-shaped sugar cake to an ice cream man who had run out of paper dishes. The author has elaborated on this information to produce an enjoyable story for young readers.

All of the 312 words used in *The Ice Cream Cone* are listed. Regular possessives and contractions ('s, n't, 'll), regular verb forms (-s, -ed, -ing), and plurals of words already on the list are not listed separately, but the endings are given in parentheses after the word.

5 one	happened	from	hard
long-ago	that	every	for
summertime	boy	state (s)	sugar
a	named	and	cake (s)
world ('s)	Jemal	sixty	on
fair	work (ed) (s)	country (ies)	an
was	at	they	open (ed)
held	he	to	fire
in	help (er)	see (ing)	so
the	bake (r) (s) (d)	new	everyone
city	Mr.	things	could
of	Hamwi	show (ed)	watch (ed)
St. Louis	had	off	**7** shop
Missouri	come	their	next
people	call (ed)	wares	ice cream
came	Syria	**6** it	stand

30

very	line (s)	told	crowded
soon	wait (ing)	go (ing)	who
man	ask (ed)	job	why
Frank	how	has	ordered
two	we	**10** sad (ly)	six
become	make (r)	but	more
good	these	glad	ten
friend (s) ('s)	buy	get (ting)	box (es)
when	our	front	paper
busy	I ('ll)	girl	dish (es)
day	will	hurry	spoons
done	out	please	factory
sat	said	me	**14** fast (er)
together	taste	or	bumped
ate	treat	miss	elbows
up	special	hundred	reached
leftover (s)	king ('s)	automobile (s)	again
always	table	**12** driver (s)	**15** pile (d)
lots	cared	started	grew
look (ed) (ing)	what	trip	smaller
bottom	**9** smile	New York City	finally
can (s)	no	crossed	use (d)
find	not	many	last
any	earn	all	must
8 most	enough	way	back
passed	money	would	**16** through
right	pay	end	empty
by	his	with	been
instead	rent	parade	too
stood	running	**13** invent (ion) (ed)	notice
long (er)	flour	be	**17** far

away
maybe
lost
19 bring
some
walked
frowning
if
sell
sun
turn
into
soup
were
packed
melt (ed)
scoop (s)
put
sign
closed
20 do (n't)
you
have
glass (es)
never
wash
then
this
is
big
surely

someone
extra
21 first
stopped
cotton
candy
my
rolled-up
pieces
22 place (s)
where
full
bright
light (s)
inside
here
learn
electric
am
now
23 suddenly
street
banging
popping
coat
dusty
wearing
cap
24 give
ride
thank

able
your
25 feet
hurt
head
whirling
around
eyes
tried
wish
wanted
saw
something
else
take
idea
26 found
still
almost
irons
cold
just
like
picked
cone-shaped
fill (ed)
cones
honey
fruit
today
bothered

anything
whole
basket
them
each
hold
second
top
28 cried
him
without
stir
mix
batter
need
ran
forth
between
happy
tomorrow
let's
business
29 after
loved
whenever
there
liked
chocolate
strawberry
four